To my husband Larry,
for all his love and inspiration.

Parent's Introduction

We Both Read is the first series of books designed to invite parents and children to share the reading of a story by taking turns reading aloud. This "shared reading" innovation, which was developed in conjunction with early reading specialists, invites parents to read the more sophisticated text on the left-hand pages, while children are encouraged to read the right-hand pages, which have been written at one of three early reading levels.

Reading aloud is one of the most important activities parents can share with their child to assist their reading development. However, *We Both Read* goes beyond reading *to* a child and allows parents to share reading *with* a child. *We Both Read* is so powerful and effective because it combines two key elements in learning: "showing" (the parent reads) and "doing" (the child reads). The result is not only faster reading development for the child, but a much more enjoyable and enriching experience for both!

Most of the words used in the child's text should be familiar to them. Others can easily be sounded out. An occasional difficult word will be first introduced in the parent's text, distinguished with **bold lettering**. Pointing out these words, as you read them, will help familiarize them to your child. You may also find it helpful to read the entire book aloud yourself the first time, then invite your child to participate on the second reading. Also note that the parent's text is preceded by a "talking parent" icon: ☺ ; and the child's text is preceded by a "talking child" icon: ☺ .

We Both Read books is a fun, easy way to encourage and help your child to read — and a wonderful way to start your child off on a lifetime of reading enjoyment!

We Both Read: Hansel and Gretel

We Both Read® is a trademark of Treasure Bay, Inc.

Published by Treasure Bay, Inc.
17 Parkgrove Drive
South San Francisco, CA 94080 USA

PRINTED IN SINGAPORE

Library of Congress Catalog Card Number: 98-61765

Hardcover ISBN 1-891327-13-5
Paperback ISBN 1-891327-17-8

FIRST EDITION

We Both Read® Books
Patent No. 5,957,693

Visit us online at:
www.webothread.com

WE BOTH READ™

Hansel & Gretel

Adapted by Sindy McKay
From the story by the Brothers Grimm
Illustrated by Tim Barnes

TREASURE BAY

Once, near a great forest, there lived a poor woodcutter and his children: a boy named **Hansel** and a girl named **Gretel**. One night the woodcutter lamented, "There is little left to eat but a few crusts of bread. I fear that soon we'll all starve to death."

👀 **Hansel** and **Gretel** were up in their beds.

They heard what their father said.

They wished that they could help.

The next day the children went into the woods with their father. He warned them not to wander away, for he was **afraid** they might get **lost**. Then he gave them each the last crusts of bread and he set off to chop the nearby trees.

Hansel and Gretel did not want to starve. So Hansel took Gretel by the hand and together they went off in search of nuts and berries to eat.

Gretel was **afraid**.

She knew the woods were big.

She knew they could get **lost**.

But Hansel had a plan.

    "We each were given a crust of bread," Hansel reminded
Gretel. "We'll use it to leave a trail to lead us back to Father."
    And so the children set off into the **woods**, leaving a trail of
breadcrumbs behind them.

Hansel and Gretel looked for food.

They went deeper and deeper into the **woods**.

But they did not find any food.

Soon the moon rose in the sky, telling them it was time to go back. But when they tried to follow their trail home, they found that it had disappeared! The birds of the forest had eaten it up, leaving Hansel and Gretel lost in the woods.

Hansel and Gretel started to walk.

They walked until they could walk no more.

Then they stopped by a tree and fell asleep.

 Hansel and Gretel woke the next morning to the sound of a pretty white bird singing sweetly on the bough of a tree. The bird seemed to tell them to **follow** him.

When the bird had finished his song, he spread his wings and flew away.

Hansel and Gretel **followed** the bird.

They followed the bird through the woods.

They followed the bird to a little house.

The little house was built of gingerbread. The **roof** was shingled with sweet little cakes and the **windows** were made of transparent sugar.

Hansel and Gretel wondered how the little house would **taste**.

Hansel took a bite of the **roof**.

Gretel took a bite of the **window**.

The sweet little house **tasted** very good!

Suddenly they heard a thin voice call out from inside,
  "Nibble, nibble, little mouse,
    Who is **nibbling** at my house?"
Hansel and Gretel should have been frightened. But they
were too hungry to be scared. And so they kept eating.

 Hansel took more bites from the roof.

Gretel ate the rest of the window.

Then they both began **nibbling** on the wall.

Then the door swung open and an old **woman** stepped out, scaring Hansel and Gretel half out of their wits!

But the old woman smiled and kindly said, "Ah, my dear children, come inside with me and I will give you more to eat."

The old **woman** put out her hands.

Gretel took one hand and Hansel took the other.

Then the old woman led them inside her house.

The old woman fed them a wondrous meal, then showed them two soft little beds. Hansel and Gretel laid themselves down and, blissfully happy, drifted off to sleep.

Hansel and Gretel did not know that this old woman was really a **witch**.

All **witches** have red eyes.

This witch had red eyes too.

But Hansel and Gretel did not see that.

Early the next morning, the witch revealed herself to Hansel when she grasped him with her withered hand and yanked him from his bed.

Hansel kicked and Gretel screamed as the witch **dragged** the boy outside to a small **cage**.

The witch put Hansel inside the **cage**.

Then she **dragged** Gretel to the stove.

She made Gretel cook for her brother.

Every day the witch forced Gretel to cook huge **meals** for her brother while Gretel herself was given nothing but crabshells to eat. This the witch did to make Hansel grow fat. For once the young boy was juicy and plump, she planned to cook him and eat him up!

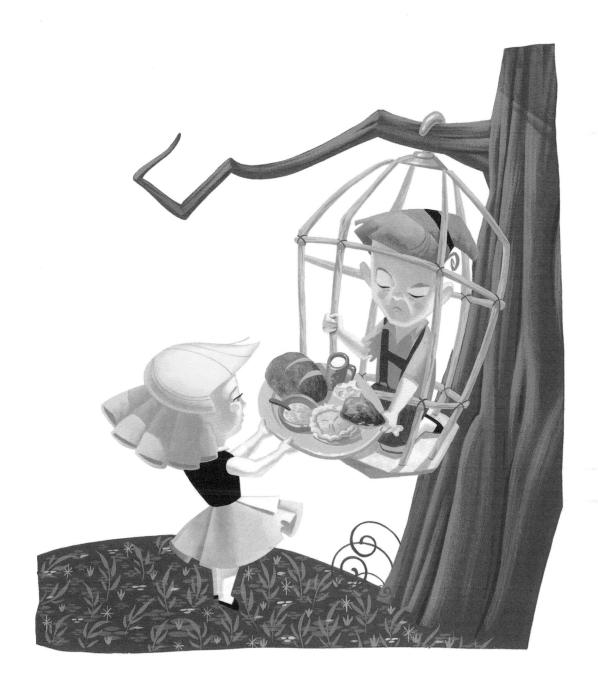

Every day Gretel brought food to her brother.

Every day Hansel shared his **meals** with his sister.

Every day the witch came to see if Hansel was fat.

The witch would ask Hansel to stick his finger out of the cage so she could feel if it was getting **plump**. But the witch had poor eyesight, as most witches do, so Hansel would hold out an old **thin** bone instead. The witch, with her weak eyes, did not know the difference.

This went on for a long, long time.
Then one day the witch said,
"I don't care if he is **plump** or **thin**.
It is time to eat the boy."

Oh what grief for poor Gretel when the witch dragged her to the oven and demanded that she stoke the fire!

And when the flames were shining bright, the witch smiled at Gretel and said, "My dear, **peek** inside the **oven** door and see if the fire is properly hot."

Gretel did not want to **peek** inside the **oven**.

Gretel knew what the witch would do.

She knew the witch would push her in.

She knew the witch would eat her up too!

So instead of peeking, Gretel said, "I'm sorry, ma'am. I don't **understand**; how is it that I should peek in?"

"Stupid goose," said the nasty old witch, "just **lean** inside the oven door."

Gretel said, "I still don't **understand**."

And again the witch said, "**Lean** inside!"

Gretel said, "Could you show me, please?"

Frustrated and angry, the witch screamed at Gretel. "Just poke your head inside the door!"

The witch stooped over and leaned inside the oven's **huge iron** mouth. "Like this, you goose. Now do you see?"

Gretel gave her a great big push!

She pushed the witch right into the oven!

Then she shut the **huge iron** door!

And that was the end of *that* old witch.

Gretel raced to Hansel's cage and threw open the door to release her brother!

"Hansel, we are free!" she cried. "The wicked old witch is dead!"

Hansel hugged his sister.

Gretel kissed her brother.

Hansel and Gretel were so happy to be free!

And so, as they had nothing more to fear, the children explored the old witch's house, and in every corner they found chests of pearls and precious stones. Hansel filled his pockets until they bulged and Gretel filled her apron to nearly bursting!

Hansel and Gretel left the house.

It was time to try to get back home.

They began to walk into the woods.

As Hansel and Gretel walked farther and farther into the woods, the way **began** to grow more familiar. Their pace quickened as their confidence grew. At last, in the distance they saw their father's house.

Hansel and Gretel **began** to run.

They ran all the way to their father's house.

They ran into their father's arms.

The **woodcutter** cried tears of joy as he held his children in a warm embrace. At last his family was **together** again!

Gretel opened her apron to let the precious stones spill out while Hansel happily took handfuls of pearls from his pockets and threw them in the air!

Hansel and Gretel were glad to be home.

The **woodcutter** was glad his children were back.

From that day on, they lived **together** in joy.

If you liked
Hansel and Gretel, **here are other**
We Both Read™ **Books you are sure to enjoy!**

In this humorous and charming tale, a princess
loses her golden ball and then makes promises to the
frog who gets it back for her. But the princess does not
want to keep her promises! To her surprise the frog
appears at the castle door looking for the princess and
all that she promised!

This lively retelling of the classic story is filled with humor and excitement. Much to his mother's dismay, Jack trades their only cow for five beans. But from these beans grows a magic beanstalk, which Jack climbs up to confront a fearsome giant. Jack must outwit and outrun the giant to reclaim his family's golden treasures!

In this delightfully funny retelling of the classic
story, the emperor hires two tailors to make him an
elegant new set of clothes. The tailors say the clothes
are magical and that some people will think the
clothes are invisible. Can you guess what happens
when the emperor wears his new clothes?